SNOW TRACKS

SNOW TRACKS

Story and Pictures by
JEAN GEORGE

E. P. Dutton & Co., Inc. – New York

To

JOHN CRAIGHEAD GEORGE

who at four and one-half could write hunting stories

in the snow

SNOW TRACKS

The snow sprinkled out of
the sky one day until the floor
of the February woodland was as smooth and white as
paper. The snow stopped falling in the late afternoon.

For more than an hour the woodland was black and
white and silent.

At half past five, a bird's nest rustled on its twig. The wind had not stirred it.

At twenty to six, the roof of grass on the nest lifted and a hazelnut rolled out. It plopped onto the snow, where it lay covered with messages to the woodland. Some of the messages were odors, some of the messages were teeth marks. Together they told that the hazelnut had just been held and chewed and opened and eaten by a fat old white-footed mouse.

At ten to six, the roof of the nest lifted again, and there sat the fat old white-footed mouse. This was Chief Half-an-Ear, the cautious, wise chief of the streamland mice.

He looked at the hazelnut; he looked at the sky, and he sniffed the woodland floor. Then he rushed down his tree. Little niceties like looking before he rushed had made Chief Half-an-Ear the oldest mouse in the woodland— two and a half years old.

Chief Half-an-Ear stepped on the white, smooth snow and began to write with his feet and tail. His snow prints read like this:

"The snow is so deep that my tail drags, and I cannot run fast. There are no more seeds in my storeroom in the stump. I plod on.

"There are acorns, maple keys and beechnuts in my cache under the tree root. I eat an acorn. I walk on, for I smell something under the snow."

Here the mouse writing ends.

The weasel in the weasel den awoke and sniffed the air. Then his eyelids closed as he fell asleep again; this time he was only half asleep, not in the deep faraway sleep of the weasel. His nose twitched; his body tensed; his eyes opened again. He was awake and up. He flashed to the door of his den and tasted the odors on the wind. He did not smell the cardinal sleeping in the hemlock, or the juncos roosting in the blackberry thicket.

The weasel dove into the snow as if it were water, tunneled through it and came up five feet away. He bounced along on top of the snow, dove down for another plunge, and stopped at the hazelnut. He read all the messages written on it, and turned to follow the chief of the mice.

The weasel wrote this:

"I am tracking that delicious old Chief Half-an-Ear. Ha!"

He followed Half-an-Ear to the stump cache. He tracked
him to the tree roots. Two leaps farther, he read in the
snow that Chief Half-an-Ear was gone.

Out from his den near the stream came another snow writer. He was writing this:

"I am large. I am fearless. I walk under the barred owl. I find the diving, sliding weasel trail and I pursue the weasel. Ah, he is following the fat old mouse chief, so I shall track them both. I walk steadily and slowly without fear, for I am the skunk."

The skunk stopped in confusion. The mouse track had disappeared.

The skunk read the sign. He read where the weasel had dived in and out of the snow. The skunk dug down to the moss, but still he could not find the mouse chief. He plodded around and around the spot where the mouse had disappeared. Something strange had happened to Chief Half-an-Ear. The skunk decided to track the weasel up the stream to see if he had found any fresh messages from the mouse.

The skunk saw the weasel thrust his head out of the snow and bound to the fan-like snow prints of the owl. The weasel sniffed the prints and read that the owl had caught a mouse; but it was a young and tender mouse, not old Chief Half-an-Ear.

The skunk plodded on looking for Half-an-Ear. He
found another scent in the snow. It smelled of the cotton-
tail rabbit that had bounced away when the weasel slipped
past.

25

Through the dark woods came another snow writer. His snow prints danced and cavorted. He left nose holes that told where he had sniffed into the snow and snorted.

His tracks met the skunk tracks; he followed the skunk tracks to the weasel tracks; the weasel tracks to the mouse tracks.

His tracks were gay tracks which might have been read
to say:

"Look at all these interesting remarks in the snow.
Everybody is after old Chief Half-an-Ear."

Then his tracks went around and around in circles as
he too, searched for the missing chief of the mice.

27

Clown-face, the raccoon, made a stomach print in the snow as he all but buried himself, sniffing and hunting for the delicious Chief Half-an-Ear.

He rubbed the snow in his hands and tasted it, for he thought he smelled peanut butter. Being an animal of sophisticated tastes that often took him to trash cans, he knew all about peanut butter.

He found neither mouse, nor peanut butter, so he followed the skunk and the weasel in their search for Chief Half-an-Ear.

Suddenly all the snow tracks read:
"Run! Run! Run, for your life!"

The raccoon galloped up a tree, passed the tracks of the squirrel, and crossed the thin branches to another tree, to lose his trail in the air.

The skunk lifted his tail and stood ready to fire!

The weasel slipped under the snow and vanished in a
pile of fallen limbs.

The feared animal was nearing the woods. His tracks
lay in single file behind him. He had been at the barn,
had circled the chicken coop and had gone under the fence
by the silo.

The tracks had changed when he had galloped across
the open field.

The snow tracks circled the hemlock where the cardinal was sleeping. They were pressed back and forth at the base of the blackberry thicket where the juncos were nestled from the cold.

They led right to the grass clump where a pheasant had
roosted.

Deep wing prints in the snow told of the frightened
flight of the bird.

The tracks stalked on. In single file they entered the woodland. They circled the snow prints of the raccoon, and pounced on the tracks of the skunk.

They hurried along the trail of the weasel and stopped
at the spot where Chief Half-an-Ear had disappeared.

Over that mysterious spot stood the tawny-eyed red fox!

The fox poked his nose in the snow at the end of the
mouse trail and his red tongue flashed over his teeth. No
mouse! Only the scent of peanut butter.

The fox twisted his big, sound-gathering ears and listened. He darted to cover under the folded laurel leaves. His tracks were twenty feet apart—leaping, frightened tracks.

The scent he left behind drifted to the noses of the raccoon, the skunk, and the weasel. It bore the taint of fright.

The hidden snow writers threw off their scents of fright as they sought deeper cover. The odor of the next snow writer had reached the forest before him.

This animal had also begun his snow writing at the
farmhouse. He had come across the trail of the fox and
had followed him around the barn.

He had tracked him to the chicken coop and out under
the fence.

He had followed the fox to the hemlock where the cardinal was sleeping, and to the berry bush where the juncos roosted.

He found bird prints where the juncos had hopped
before going to roost.

Then he tracked the fox to the woods, where he found the snow tracks of the raccoon, the skunk, and the weasel. Presently he discovered the tiny little prints of Chief Half-an-Ear.

Over the spot where the chief had vanished loomed a trapper. He looked at all the writing on the snow, and said aloud:

"It certainly has been a busy night out here."

He looked around once more and observed that every-
one who had been hunting was now hiding.

The trapper had come to the woods on business. He leaned down where the trail of Chief Half-an-Ear ended and carefully pushed back the snow. He dug up his little box trap that could catch an animal alive. He had buried it carefully in the chief's secret trail that led from his nest to the water. The trapper had been pleased with his cleverness. He was more pleased when he looked in the box.

"Hooray, and tally-ho!" he shouted.

Nestled in the warm cotton in the trap sat Chief Half-an-Ear, stuffing on peanut butter.

The trapper did not stand still long. The next thing that was written in the snow were his very fastest running prints.

The trapper was making tracks that led to the farm-house as fast as he could print them. The trapper was very frightened.

An enormous snow writer was following the footsteps of the trapper.

The enormous prints stopped where the trap had been. They told that the great animal had torn the snow to the bare ground, had snuffed up snow and dirt, and then had lunged on down the trapper's trail.

It was the great black bear of the forest who was hungry for a little taste of peanut butter. He slashed a tree to exercise his nails, sniffed the dog prints and cat prints that had been left by a running dog and fleeing cat, and followed the trapper.

He stopped at the edge of the woods and watched the trapper making tracks across the field. He did not follow him any more, for he had been sleeping all winter and was still not wide awake. He just sniffed the last odor of peanut butter on the wind and turned sadly away.

The big old snow writer circled back to his den and scratched his head on his log until he fell fast asleep.

In all the hidden burrows, dens and holes, small eyes were upon the bear and twisting ears were listening in his direction. When his breathing became almost silent, the fox, the raccoon, the skunk and the weasel slipped down into their sleeping holes and the story writers went to sleep.

Across the field at the farmhouse, the kitchen door banged shut and the trapper locked it tight. Then he wrote a message to his mother on the floor and table with wet footprints and other things. It said:

"I have been in the woods. I am safe now. I have been to the cupboard for peanut butter and jelly, and to the refrigerator for milk.

"I have taken off my coat and boots, and I am in my room admiring the soft, twitching face and bright eyes of this little wild thing I have brought from the forest."

Chief Half-an-Ear was placed in a fine cage filled with cotton, water and food. He settled down happily to house building. Then he tasted his new exciting foods, and hopped in and out of his nest without a worry in his head. Here there was no fox, no raccoon, no skunk, no weasel. He looked forward to the ripe old age for a mouse of four or even five.

At dawn the snow circled out of the sky and fell silently
on the woodland floor. By seven o'clock in the morning,
it had erased the story in the snow. The new snow lay
smooth, like white paper, over the land.

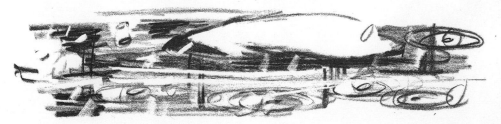